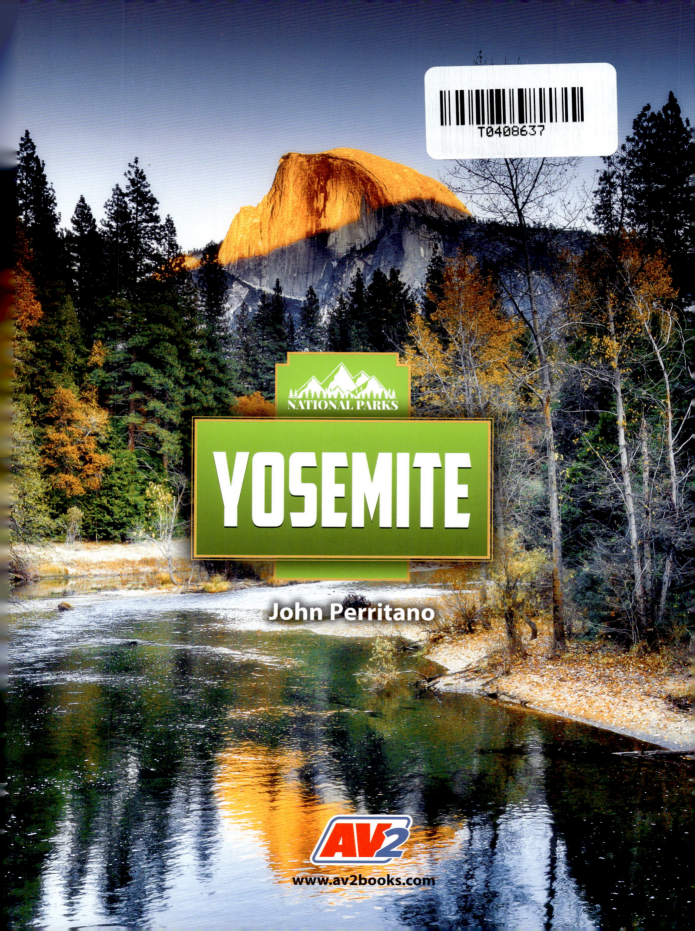

NATIONAL PARKS

YOSEMITE

John Perritano

AV2
www.av2books.com

Step 1
Go to www.av2books.com

Step 2
Enter this unique code
YXPUONIU8

Step 3
Explore your interactive eBook!

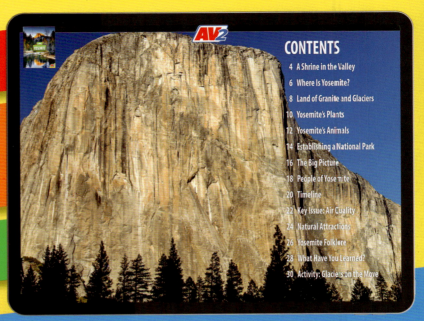

AV2 is optimized for use on any device

Your interactive eBook comes with...

Contents
Browse a live contents page to easily navigate through resources

Audio
Listen to sections of the book read aloud

Videos
Watch informative video clips

Weblinks
Gain additional information for research

Try This!
Complete activities and hands-on experiments

Key Words
Study vocabulary, and complete a matching word activity

Quizzes
Test your knowledge

Slideshows
View images and captions

... and much, much more!

NATIONAL PARKS
YOSEMITE

CONTENTS

AV2 Book Code 2

A Shrine in the Valley 4

Where Is Yosemite? 6

Land of Granite and Glaciers . . . 8

Yosemite's Plants 10

Yosemite's Animals 12

Establishing a National Park . . . 14

The Big Picture 16

People of Yosemite 18

Timeline 20

Key Issue:
Air Quality 22

Natural Attractions 24

Yosemite Folklore 26

What Have You Learned? 28

Activity:
Glaciers on the Move 30

Key Words/Index 31

Yosemite 3

A Shrine in the Valley

With its tall granite peaks, towering waterfalls, and giant sequoia trees, Yosemite National Park is a feast for the eyes. It is no wonder that more than 4 million people visit the park every year. Natural wonders can be seen around every corner.

However, at one time, the scenic beauty of the land was overlooked. People moved to the area to settle the land. Farmers let their animals graze in the fields. Logging companies began to cut down trees. **Naturalists** fought to restore the land to its natural state.

Yosemite was the **3rd** national park in American history.

Almost **75 percent** of the tourists that visit Yosemite do so between May and October.

The giant sequoia trees in Yosemite are more than **3,000 years** old.

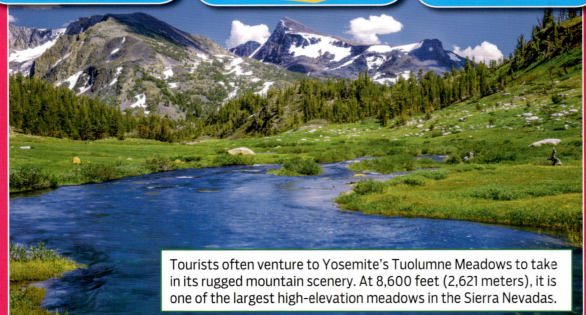

Tourists often venture to Yosemite's Tuolumne Meadows to take in its rugged mountain scenery. At 8,600 feet (2,621 meters), it is one of the largest high-elevation meadows in the Sierra Nevadas.

Today, Yosemite consists of 1,169 square miles (3,028 square kilometers) of natural splendor. Coniferous forests blanket the ground, while the stark majesty of the Sierra Nevada mountains rise above the **tree line**. The diverse landscape attracts a variety of animals, ranging from tiny insects to large **mammals**.

Early park promoters carved tunnels into some of the larger sequoias to attract tourists. Some of these trees remain standing today.

MAPPING YOSEMITE

LEGEND
- California
- Yosemite
- Nevada
- Mexico
- City
- Water

MAP SCALE 0 — 100 Miles / 100 Km

N

Where Is Yosemite?

Yosemite National Park is located in east-central California, close to the Nevada border. There are five entrances to the park. Four are found along the park's west side. The other entrance is on the east side.

The park is situated within the Sierra Nevadas. These mountains extend more than 400 miles (644 km) along California's eastern border. Yosemite is bordered by national forests on all sides. The Sierra National Forest is southeast of the park. Stanislaus National Forest lies to the northwest. Inyo National Forest is due east. The town nearest to Yosemite is Oakhurst. It is located about 16 miles (26 km) south of the park.

The peaks of the Sierra Nevadas range in height from 11,000 to 14,000 feet (3,353 to 4,267 m).

PUZZLER

The Sierra Nevadas are just one of many mountain ranges found in the United States.

Q: Can you identify each of these mountain ranges?

HINT: This mountain range's highest mountain is Mount Elbert. It stands at a height of 14,440 feet (4,401 m).

HINT: The highest peak in this mountain range is North Carolina's Mount Mitchell. It is 6,684 feet (2,037 m) in height.

HINT: This mountain range is home to Denali, the highest mountain in North America.

ANSWERS: A. Rocky Mountains B. Appalachian Mountains C. Alaska Range

Yosemite 7

Land of Granite and Glaciers

The Sierra Nevadas began forming deep beneath Earth's surface about 245 million years ago. It took another 175 million years for them to break ground. Not long after the Sierras began rising, Earth cooled. Snow and ice began to fall. Over time, a series of **glaciers** formed in the highlands of what is now California. These glaciers carved out U-shaped valleys. One of these valleys would later become known as Yosemite Valley.

The glaciers finally retreated about 10,000 to 15,000 years ago, leaving behind the smooth domes of Tuolumne Meadows and the high country's jagged peaks. The granite that formed the mountains was not a giant slab of rock. Instead, it was made up of smaller chunks of granite that merged over time.

The glaciers also left behind a **terminal moraine**. This wall of rock and sediment formed a dam across Yosemite Valley. As the years passed, water gathered behind the dam, creating Yosemite Lake. The lake was eventually replaced by meadows and forests.

As the glaciers receded, they left behind large rocks called erratics. Some of the best examples of erratics in Yosemite can be found at Olmsted Point, just north of Yosemite Valley.

ICY REMAINS

Only two glaciers are left in Yosemite. The Lyell and Maclure glaciers formed about 400 years ago, during what scientists call the Little **Ice Age**. Both ice sheets are important to the park's **ecosystem**. This is because they fill the Tuolumne River and the Lyell Fork with a constant supply of water.

Explorers first mapped and photographed the ice sheets in 1883. Scientists still study the glaciers because they provide insight into the health of the park. Within the last 10 years, the glaciers have been melting at a rapid pace. Scientists believe that this is a result of **global warming**.

The Tuolumne River is about 150 miles (241 km) long. It begins at Mount Lyell, in Yosemite, and empties into the San Joaquin River, California's second-longest river.

The Lyell Glacier is only 20 percent of the size it was in the 1800s. About 3 feet (90 centimeters) of thickness are melting away every year.

Yosemite's Plants

Yosemite teems with a variety of **vegetation**. The giant sequoia tree is its best-known plant. Located in three areas of the park, the sequoias are one of the longest-living tree **species** in the Western Hemisphere.

These sequoias are also the largest known trees on the planet. They can grow to be about 250 feet (76 m) tall and 30 feet (9 m) in diameter. About 500 mature trees can be found in the southern portion of Yosemite, in Mariposa Grove.

While the sequoias reach up toward the sky, other plants stay much closer to the ground. Approximately 1,450 species of wildflowers grow in the park, and blossoms can be found year-round. Chief among them is the monkey flower. About 32 species of monkey flowers are located here. Some grow at lower elevations. Others can only be found on the mountainsides. Lupines, poppies, and lilies are just some of the other wildflowers found in the park.

Monkey flowers are very resilient and are capable of living in a variety of environments. They can be found growing in sandy or rocky terrain, wet or dry soil, and in either direct sunlight or shade.

VEGETATION ZONES

Yosemite has several vegetation zones, or areas where specific plants grow. These zones showcase the park's varied ecosystem and climate.

Foothill-Woodland Zone Located at lower elevations, this zone is often hot and dry. Plants such as the blue oak grow here, as well as an evergreen shrub with narrow leaves, called the chamise.

Lower Montane Forest This zone begins at elevations of about 3,000 feet (914 m). Here, summers are dry and winters are wet, providing prime growing conditions for many tree species, including the sequoia.

Upper Montane Forest Starting at elevations of about 6,000 feet (1,829 m), this zone can receive up to 6 feet (1.8 m) of snow in the winter. Red firs, Jeffrey pines, and western junipers thrive here.

Subalpine Forest Appearing at elevations of about 8,000 feet (2,438 m), this zone's climate is cool and snowy. Hemlock and pine trees grow here. However, their growth is often stunted due to the cold.

Alpine Zone This zone sits above the tree line, starting at an elevation of about 9,500 feet (2,900 m). Known for its harsh climate, only small, hardy plants are able to survive here.

Yosemite's Animals

Much like its landscape, Yosemite's wildlife is also diverse. The park is home to 262 species of birds, 90 mammal species, and 22 species of reptiles. This diversity is a result of the park's many habitats. Some animals, such as black bears, dwell in meadows, where it is easy to **forage**. Others, such as Sierra Nevada bighorn sheep, prefer rocky mountainsides, where few **predators** dare to go.

The park's waters are home to a variety of fish. These include the riffle sculpin and the hardhead. The western pond turtle, Yosemite's only turtle species, resides in watery areas as well. The Sierra garter snake is often found near water. The northern Pacific rattlesnake lives in dry, rocky locales.

Yosemite is a birdwatcher's paradise. People come to the park to spot favorites such as the acorn woodpecker and the mountain bluebird. On rare occasions, they may see a golden eagle soaring high above the trees.

The bobcat is the smallest wildcat found in Yosemite. It preys on animals such as rabbits, squirrels, and mice.

RETURN OF THE BIGHORN

Sierra Nevada bighorn sheep roamed Yosemite long before the area became a national park. However, their numbers declined greatly when settlers arrived. Hunters sought the animals for food. Farm animals brought diseases that the sheep were unable to fight. The bighorns disappeared from the area within 24 years of Yosemite being named a national park. The only sheep from this **subspecies** to remain were found in the southern part of the mountain range.

In 1981, a movement began to bring bighorns back to Yosemite. Five years later, a herd of 27 sheep was placed near the park's western border. Over time, the number of bighorns grew. Today, more than 600 Sierra Nevada bighorn sheep live inside the park.

The Sierra Nevada bighorn sheep can be identified by its horns. While the horns of other bighorn sheep have a tight curl, the Sierra Nevada's horns extend out in an arc.

Establishing a National Park

Until 1848, Native Americans were the only people living in the Yosemite Valley. That year, gold was discovered in the area. Thousands of people moved to the region, hoping to strike it rich. The California Gold Rush was on.

Settlers came to the area soon after. Native Americans had to compete with them for land. In 1851, a war broke out between the two groups. When it was over, more settlers arrived. Tourists soon followed. The influx of people began to take its toll on the pristine beauty of the land.

The California Gold Rush lasted from 1848 until 1857. It is estimated that more than 300,000 people came to the state in search of wealth and a better life.

A group of **conservationists** met with President Abraham Lincoln. They asked him to protect the valley from further harm. Lincoln agreed and signed the Yosemite Valley Grant Act in 1864. This put much of the area under the protection of the state of California.

The land outside this area was still being destroyed by human use, however. John Muir was one of many people that started campaigning to make Yosemite a national park. In 1890, Congress granted their wish.

BIOGRAPHY

John Muir (1838–1914)

While many people worked hard to establish a national park in the Yosemite Valley, none are more closely linked to the cause than John Muir. Born in Scotland in 1838, Muir moved to the United States with his parents in 1849. He and his younger brother often hiked the fields near their Wisconsin home. As they did, Muir fell in love with nature. That love ultimately took him to Yosemite.

Muir visited the area for the first time in 1868. He came back the next year and took on a series of jobs. When he had time, Muir wrote about the nature he saw around him. His work was eventually published in newspapers and magazines across the country.

Over time, Muir became concerned about the effects that humans were having on the Yosemite Valley. His writings began to reflect these concerns. The campaign to make Yosemite a national park stemmed from his writings.

FACTS OF LIFE

Born: April 21, 1838
Hometown: Dunbar, Scotland
Occupation: Naturalist
Died: December 24, 1914

THE BIG PICTURE

Yosemite National Park is home to many unique rock formations. El Capitan and Half Dome are two of its most recognizable natural landmarks. Both are **monoliths**. El Capitan is a massive outcropping of granite, extending to a height of 3,000 feet (914 m). Half Dome has a sheer granite face and a dome top. Monoliths can be found in various parts of the world. The largest are the best known and most visited.

North America

Atlantic Ocean

Pacific Ocean

South America

Southern Ocean

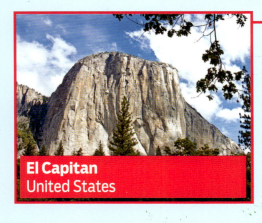
El Capitan
United States

Half Dome
United States

LEGEND
- Water
- Land
- Antarctica

N

MAP SCALE 0 — 2,000 Miles / 2,000 Km

16   National Parks

People of Yosemite

The Ahwahneechee were among the original inhabitants of the Yosemite Valley. They had lived there for thousands of years before Europeans arrived. For much of the year, the Ahwahneechee resided in villages along the Sierra Nevada foothills. Their homes were simple huts, made of thatch, bark, and earth. In the summer, some established hunting sites at higher elevations.

The Ahwahneechee were not farmers. They did not grow crops or raise domestic animals. Instead, they were fishers, hunters, and foragers, relying on the foods found in the natural environment.

When European settlers came to Yosemite, they forced many Ahwahneechee onto **reservations**. Still, some of the Ahwahneechee continued to live in the valley, with many becoming park employees. Today, Ahwahneechee people continue to work in the park as guides and interpreters.

The Ahwahneechee called their homeland Ahwahnee to reflect its deep valley. *Ahwahnee* means "Place like a Gaping Mouth."

18 National Parks

PUZZLER

The Ahwahneechee were highly skilled in using the natural resources they found. Some of their homes were built in permanent villages and occupied throughout the year. Others were summer villages.

Q. Why did the Ahwahneechee build their huts, or O'chums, in a cone-like shape with one room?

ANSWER: The shape of the hut prevented snow and rain from damaging the structure. The hut, because of its one room, was easy to keep warm with a small fire.

TIMELINE

400 million years ago
The area where the Sierra Nevada mountains now stand is covered by ocean waters.

8,000 years ago
The first humans begin to settle in the Yosemite Valley.

- 400 million years ago
- 200 million years ago
- 10,000 years ago
- 5,000 years ago

248–213 million years ago
Sediments that have accumulated over time begin to form mountain ranges.

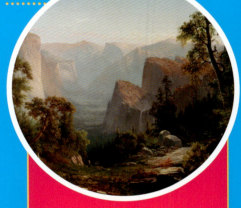

15,000–10,000 years ago
The last of the glaciers retreat, carving the valley even deeper.

1.8 million–8,000 years ago
During the Great Ice Age, a series of uplifts pushes the Sierra Nevadas up to 14,000 feet (4,267 m). Glaciers emerge in the Yosemite Valley.

1984
The **United Nations** declares Yosemite National Park a UNESCO World Heritage Site. This helps to protect it from further damage.

1830

1860

1890

2015

1833
Fur trappers cross the Sierra Nevada mountains, traveling through what would later become Yosemite National Park.

1890
Yosemite becomes a national park.

1868
John Muir arrives in Yosemite for the first time.

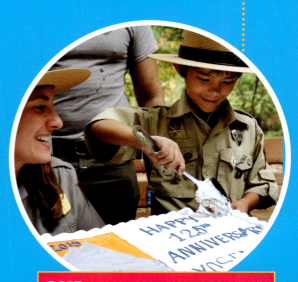

2015
Yosemite National Park celebrates its 125th anniversary.

Yosemite 21

KEY ISSUE

AIR QUALITY

One of the key issues Yosemite has faced in recent years is air quality. This issue has arisen from two main sources. First is the smoke and dust from wildfires. The second is the burning of fossil fuels, such as oil and gasoline, in areas west of the park. Both are tied to humans and how they treat the environment.

Compared to other states, California produces less fossil fuel emissions from vehicles and power plants. Yet, winds from the west can blow airborne particles eastward to the Yosemite Valley. Here, the particles linger in the air, causing breathing problems for people in the park and covering many park sites with haze and smog. This pollution can also damage the soil and surface water, as well as the plants that rely on them to survive.

Air tankers are often called to help fight forest fires in Yosemite and its surrounding areas.

Should forest fires be left to burn on their own?

Yes	No
Fires keep a forest healthy. They provide nutrients that allow trees and other vegetation to flourish. Putting out fires disrupts the natural cycle of the forest.	A forest fire can ruin an ecosystem. When vegetation is destroyed, animals have less to eat. They must move to other areas to survive.
Forest fires clear the land of dead trees and dry underbrush, which can fuel more massive and dangerous fires.	Timber is a prized **commodity**. Trees must be saved to support the forestry industry.
Fighting forest fires is expensive. In 2017 alone, the United States spent more than $2 billion fighting forest fires.	Fires can kill humans and animals, and destroy property. People can lose their homes if efforts are not made to stop a fire.

Fires can be started by humans or by nature. The result remains the same. Smoke covers the park, and air quality is impacted. In some cases, the smoke cover keeps ozone, a caustic gas, from rising. It stays close to the ground, harming plants, animals, and humans. In 2018, scientists said a massive wildfire burning on the western edge of Yosemite caused so much air pollution that the air quality in Yosemite was worse than in the city of Beijing, China. Beijing's air quality is known to be among the worst in the world.

Park managers have developed various ways to control wildfires in Yosemite. However, there is much debate about whether these actions are helping or harming the park. Some people see advantages to wildfires. Others do not.

Natural Attractions

Yosemite is an ideal place for people who love the outdoors. Visitors can go camping, fishing, rock climbing, rafting, and horseback riding. The park's campgrounds can accommodate more than 9,000 people, allowing visitors to plan multi-day stays.

Hiking trails can be found throughout the park. One of the most popular places to hike is Mariposa Grove. The grove has four main hiking trails. For the more adventurous, the El Capitan Trail takes hikers on a 15-mile (24-km) trek to the top of the mountain. From the summit, people can view many of the park's natural wonders, including Dewey Point, Half Dome, and North Dome.

Yosemite brims with waterfalls. The best-known is Yosemite Falls. At a height of 2,425 feet (739 m), it is the highest waterfall in North America and the sixth largest in the world. Horsetail Fall, just east of El Capitan, can look like it is on fire when it reflects the light of the setting Sun. The best time to see most of Yosemite's waterfalls is during the spring, when the snow starts to melt.

Yosemite Falls is made of up three separate waterfalls. They are known as the Upper Falls, the Middle Cascades, and the Lower Yosemite Fall.

HIKING YOSEMITE

Hiking is one of the best ways to see the many sights Yosemite has to offer. However, it is important that people heading out on a trail be prepared for the conditions they may encounter.

Bring Water It takes energy to hike up mountains and into valleys. As the body works, it loses fluid. Drinking water regularly keeps a hiker hydrated.

Wear Proper Footwear Hiking boots are designed to support the foot and ankle in rough terrain. They also provide good grip on loose rock and slippery slopes.

Dress in Layers The weather in Yosemite can change throughout the day and at different elevations. Wearing layered clothing ensures that hikers do not get too hot, too cold, or too wet.

Pack Food Besides carrying a nutritious lunch, hikers should always carry snacks to eat along the way. Nuts, berries, and granola all help keep a hiker's energy up as he or she navigates the trail.

Use Sun Protection To guard against sunburn, hikers should make sure they apply sunscreen before starting on the trail. More should be applied throughout the day as well.

Yosemite 25

Yosemite Folklore

Many of Yosemite's natural landmarks are steeped in Native American folklore. The myths and legends associated with Yosemite bring the land to life. They also help to explain the connection that the local Native Americans feel toward the land.

The Ahwahneechee believe that a number of spirits reside within the Yosemite Valley. One of the best known, and most dangerous, is Po-ho-no. He is said to live near Bridalveil Fall, at the southern end of the park. Visitors are warned not to get too close to the waterfall's edge. This is because Po-ho-no is said to have lured people to the water and pushed them over the falls.

Legend has it that an Ahwahneechee chief put a curse on Tenaya Canyon years ago, after his son was killed by a U.S. army battalion. With its slippery rocks, deep pools, and steep slopes, the canyon's terrain is naturally difficult. However, any time a hiker goes missing here, it is said to be because of the curse.

Tenaya Canyon is found in the shadows of Half Dome. It is about 10 miles (16 km) long, and extends from Tenaya Lake all the way to the Yosemite Valley.

LEGEND OF TUL-TOK-A-NU-LA

One of the stories handed down by the first people of Yosemite is the legend of Tul-tok-a-nu-la. Although versions can vary, it is a tale of two boys who, after a day of swimming, decided to take a nap on a large boulder. As they slept, the boulder grew larger and larger. It carried the boys high into the sky, lifting them up so high that their families and friends lost sight of them. Efforts were made to get to the boys, but no one was able to find a way to get them off the rock. People started to believe that they would never see the boys again.

A group of animals heard about what had happened and wanted to help. They banded together to see how they could get the boys off the rock. All the animals failed, except the tiny Measuring-Worm. He slowly crept up the side of the rock until he reached the top. He awakened the boys and brought them down safely. The mountain was named Tul-tok-a-nu-la, or Measuring-Worm, in his honor. Today, the mountain is better known as El Capitan.

Some Ahwahneechee called El Capitan To-tock-ah-noo-lah, which means "Rock Chief." This may have been how it was given its Spanish name, which translates to "The Captain."

WHAT HAVE YOU LEARNED?

TRUE OR FALSE?

Decide whether the following statements are true or false. If the statement is false, make it true.

1 The Ahwahneechee farmed the land in and around Yosemite.

2 There are only two glaciers left in Yosemite National Park.

3 President Abraham Lincoln signed the law designating Yosemite a national park.

4 Yosemite Falls is North America's highest waterfall.

5 More than 1,000 Sierra Nevada bighorn sheep live in the park.

6 Giant sequoias are the largest known trees on the planet.

ANSWERS
1. False. The Ahwahneechee were hunters, gatherers, and foragers.
2. True.
3. False. President Lincoln signed the Yosemite Valley Grant Act, putting much of the land under California's protection.
4. True.
5. False. The park is home to more than 600 Sierra Nevada bighorn sheep.
6. True.

SHORT ANSWER

Answer the following questions using information from the book.

1 How many bird species are found in Yosemite?

2 In what year was Yosemite designated a national park?

3 Which Yosemite canyon is said to have a curse on it?

4 What historic event started the settling of Yosemite Valley?

5 How many mature sequoia trees are in Mariposa Grove?

ANSWERS
1. 262
2. 1890
3. Tenaya Canyon
4. California Gold Rush
5. About 500

MULTIPLE CHOICE

Choose the best answer for the following questions.

1 Which mountain range runs through Yosemite National Park?

   a. Sierra Nevadas
   b. Cascade Mountains
   c. Adirondacks

2 How did John Muir express his concerns about the impact of humans on the Yosemite Valley?

   a. Paintings
   b. Writings
   c. Photographs

3 Which of the following is one of the main threats facing Yosemite National Park today?

   a. Too many tourists
   b. Water scarcity
   c. Poor air quality

4 When was the Yosemite Valley Grant Act signed?

   a. 1859
   b. 1864
   c. 1890

ANSWERS 1. a 2. b 3. c 4. b

ACTIVITY

GLACIERS ON THE MOVE

Glaciers grow when the climate is cold and melt when it warms. The constant push and pull of glaciers created Yosemite Valley and carved out its rivers, lakes, and streams. Try this activity to see how a glacier changes over time.

Materials

- Nonstick cooking spray
- 16-ounce plastic cup
- 1 cup of flour
- Gravel, dirt, and water
- Baking sheet

Instructions

1. Put the gravel and dirt in the cup until it is half full. Fill the rest of the cup with water.
2. Put the mixture into the freezer and let it sit for overnight so that it freezes into a mini glacier.
3. Once the mini glacier is frozen solid, spray the baking sheet with the cooking spray.
4. Sprinkle flour on the baking sheet to create a landscape.
5. Take the mini glacier out of the cup. Put it on the baking sheet and leave it to sit.
6. Check on the mini glacier a few times over the next few hours. What happens to the flour landscape when the glacier melts?

KEY WORDS

commodity: a product that can be bought and sold

conservationists: people who work to protect the environment

ecosystem: a community of organisms living in the same place

forage: to search widely for food

glaciers: huge sheets of snow and ice that form over time

global warming: a gradual increase in Earth's surface temperature, fueled mainly by human activities

Ice Age: a period when much of the planet was covered by glaciers

mammals: animals that have hair or fur and drink their mother's milk

monoliths: massive stone blocks made of one single piece of rock

naturalists: people who specialize in the study of nature

predators: animals that prey on other animals for food

reservations: public lands set aside for Native Americans

species: a class of animals or plants with common characteristics

subspecies: a particular type within a species

terminal moraine: a ridge of rock deposited by a glacier

tree line: the elevation at which trees stop growing

United Nations: a group of countries that work together to solve problems

vegetation: all the plants of a place

INDEX

Ahwahneechee 18, 19, 26, 27, 28

air quality 22, 23, 29

California Gold Rush 14, 29

El Capitan 16, 24, 27

forest fires 22, 23

glaciers 8, 9, 20, 28, 30

global warming 9

Lincoln, Abraham 14, 28

Muir, John 14, 15, 21, 29

sequoia trees 4, 5, 10, 11, 28, 29

Sierra Nevada bighorn sheep 12, 13, 28

Sierra Nevadas 4, 6, 7, 8, 18, 20, 21, 29

Yosemite Falls 24, 28

Yosemite 31

Get the best of both worlds.

AV2 bridges the gap between print and digital.

The expandable resources toolbar enables quick access to content including **videos**, **audio**, **activities**, **weblinks**, **slideshows**, **quizzes**, and **key words**.

Animated videos make static images come alive.

Resource icons on each page help readers to further **explore key concepts**.

Published by AV2
350 5th Avenue, 59th Floor
New York, NY 10118
Website: www.av2books.com

Copyright ©2021 AV2
All rights reserved. No part of this publication may be reproduced, stored in a retrieval system, or transmitted in any form or by any means, electronic, mechanical, photocopying, recording, or otherwise, without the prior written permission of the publisher.

Library of Congress Cataloging-ini-Publication Data
Names: Perritano, John, author.
Title: Yosemite / John Perritano and Heather Kissock.
Description: New York, NY : AV2, 2021. | Series: National parks | Includes index. | Audience: Grades 4 to 6.
Identifiers: LCCN 2019009589 (print) | LCCN 2019010874 (ebook) | ISBN 9781791110642 (Multi User Ebook)
  | ISBN 9781791110659 (Single User Ebook) | ISBN 9781791110628 (hardcover : alk. paper) | ISBN 9781791110635
  (softcover : alk. paper)
Subjects: LCSH: Yosemite National Park (Calif.)--Juvenile literature.
Classification: LCC F868.Y6 (ebook) | LCC F868.Y6 P37 2019 (print) | DDC 979.4/47--dc23
LC record available at https://lccn.loc.gov/2019009589

Printed in Guangzhou, China
1 2 3 4 5 6 7 8 9 0 24 23 22 21 20

012020
101319

Project Coordinator Heather Kissock
Designers Tammy West, Ana Maria Vidal, and Terry Paulhus
Captions Heather Kissock

Photo Credits
Every reasonable effort has been made to trace ownership and to obtain permission to reprint copyright material. The publishers would be pleased to have any errors or omissions brought to their attention so that they may be corrected in subsequent printings. AV2 acknowledges Getty Images, Alamy, iStock, and Shutterstock as its primary photo suppliers for this title.